For Matyash

In the same **Pomelo the Garden Elephant** series:

Pomelo Begins to Grow
Pomelo Explores Color

This work, published as part of a program of aid for publication,
received support from the Institut Français.
(Cet ouvrage a bénéficié du soutien des Programmes d'aide
à la publication de l'Institut français.)

First American edition published in 2013 by
Enchanted Lion Books, 20 Jay Street, Studio M-18, Brooklyn, NY 11201
Translation copyright © 2013 by Enchanted Lion Books
Translated by Claudia Zoe Bedrick
Originally published in France by Albin Michel Jeunesse © 2011 as **Pomelo et les contraires**
All rights reserved under International and Pan-American Copyright Conventions
A CIP record is on file with the Library of Congress
ISBN: 978-1-59270-132-2
Printed in February 2013 in China by South China Printing Company

Ramona Bădescu

Benjamin Chaud

Pomelo's

Opposites

ENCHANTED LION BOOKS

NEW YORK

When Pomelo
was small, he was
really small.
And he couldn't
yet see the
difference between…

closed

open

far

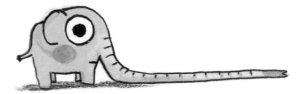

near

left

right

here

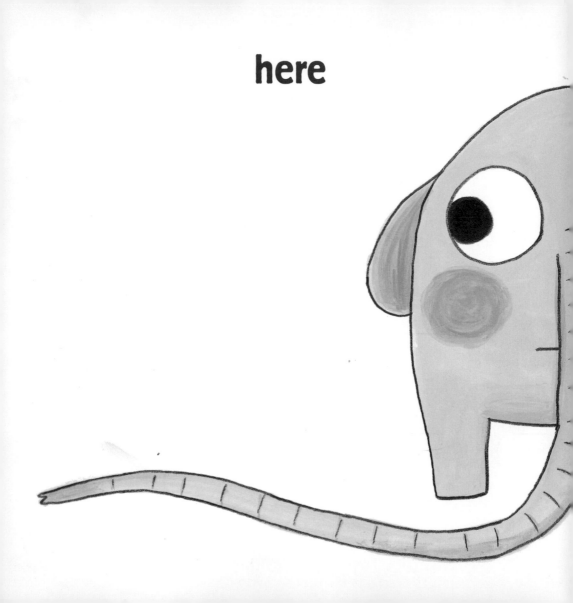

there

in front

behind

before

after

morning

evening

on

off

black

white

polka-dotted

striped

ordinary

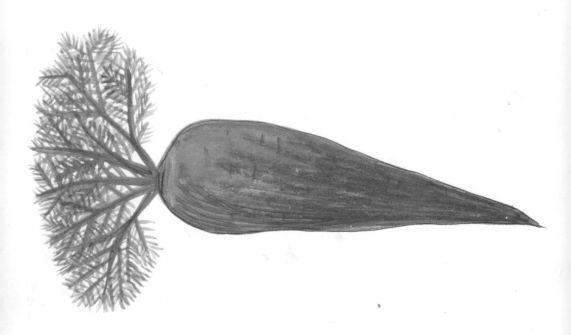

extraordinary

dressed

bare

thin

fat

in

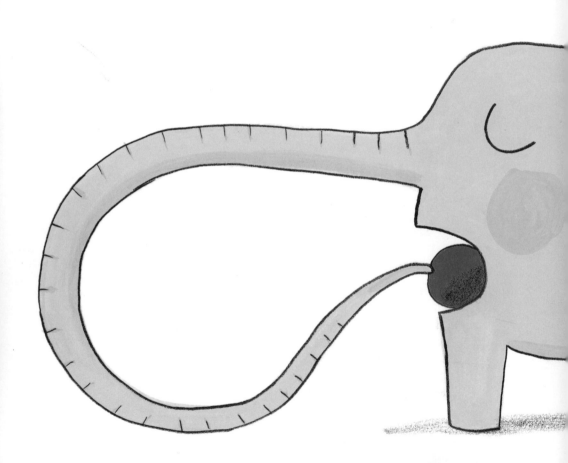

out

handsome

weird

dream

reality

possible

impossible

something

whatever

real

pretend

with

without

heartless

kind

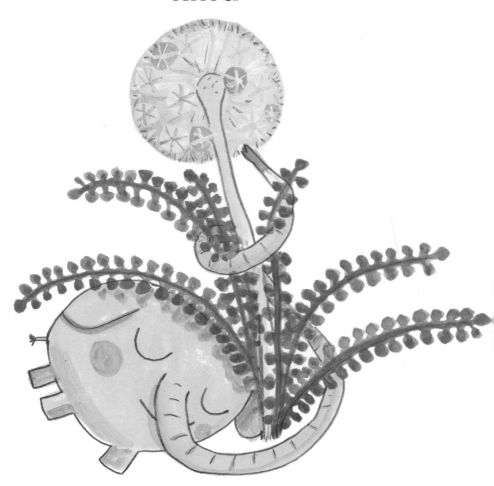

stranger

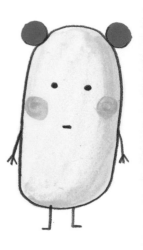

friend

see

look at

visible

invisible

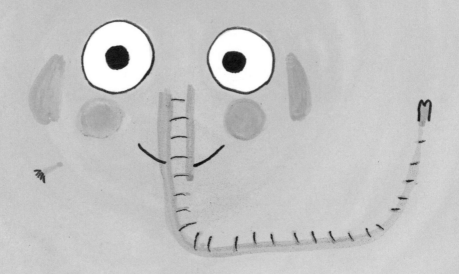

blurred

slow

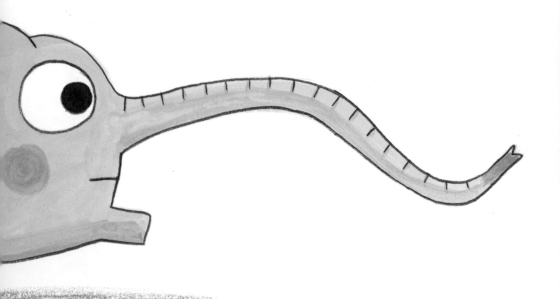

fast

on foot

by car

on snailback

by turtle

alone

together

comfortable

uncomfortable

easy

difficult

question

answer

yes

no

up

down

stalactite

stalagmite

gastropod

cucurbit

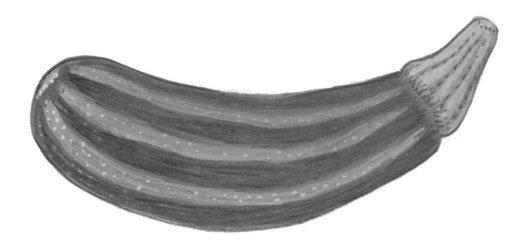

convex

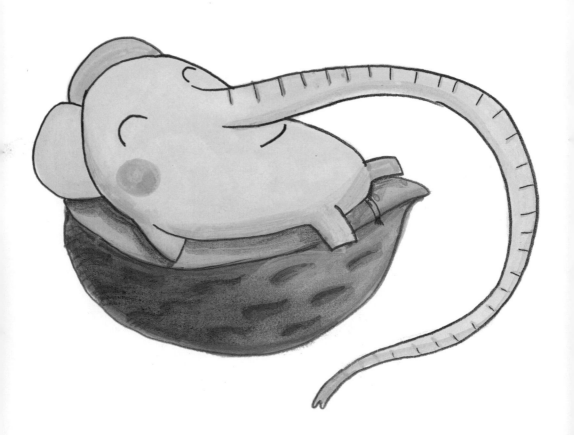

concave

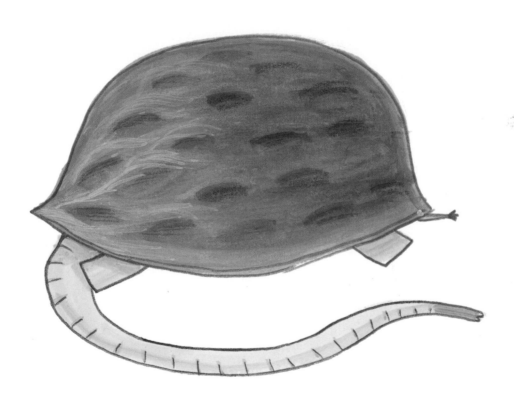

You want it?

Here it is!

one

many

having

being

full

empty

everywhere

nowhere

living

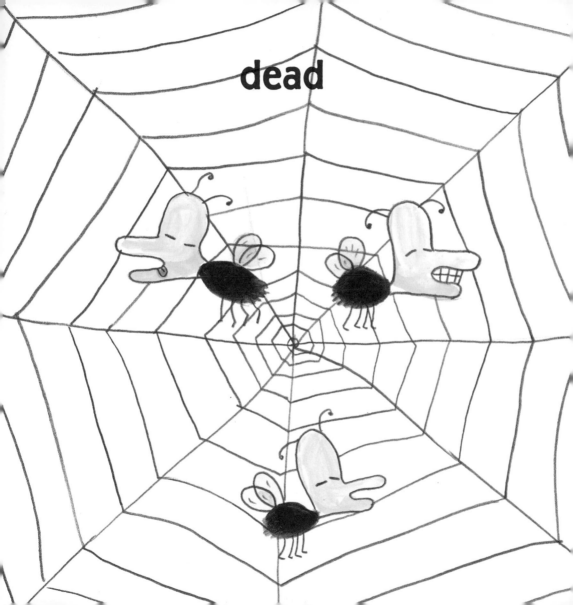

fleeting

permanent

simple

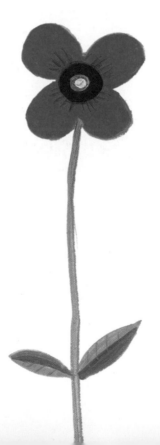

complicated

right

wrong

little

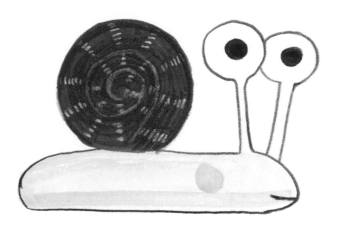

big

in the frame

outside of the frame

hard

soft

adorable

not at all adorable

sad

happy

puzzle

solution

evident

unimaginable

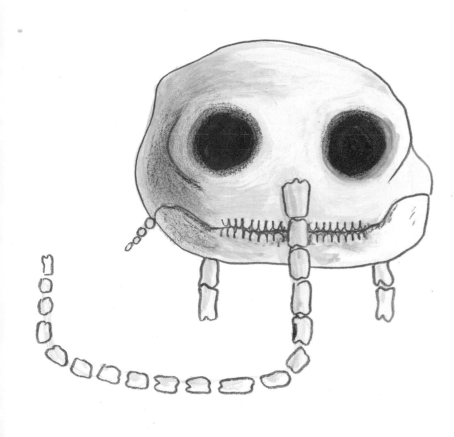

here

there

everything

nothing

scene

characters

the beginning

the end

Now that he's gotten
a little older,
Pomelo finds these
differences more
obvious, less confusing,
or maybe…
just the opposite!